SECRETS

BEYOND
THE PEWS
...Shhhh

APOSTLE LORRAINE ANDERSON

SECRETS BEYOND THE PEWS...SHHHH

APOSTLE LORRAINE ANDERSON

SECRETS BEYOND THE PEWS ... SHHHHH!

Apostle Lorraine Anderson

SECRETS BEYOND THE PEWS ... SHHHHH!

Scripture quotations are from various versions of the Holy Bible. Strong's Concordance is a viable source used, as well.

Published by Executive Business Writing
P.O. Box 10002, Moreno Valley, CA 92552
(951)268-0368
https://www.beverlycrockett.com
executivebusinesswriting@gmail.com

Edited by Julie Boney
JB Editing Solutions
www.jb-editingsolutions.com

Book covers designed by Tracy G. Spencer
Legacy Media, LLC – Moreno Valley, CA

TABLE OF CONTENTS

FOREWORD

It has been my pleasure to know and serve under the tutelage of Apostle Lorraine Anderson, a mother and mentor. Apostle Lorraine has been a minister for as long as I can remember. She has helped to reach souls with the message of faith, truth, and hope. Our relationship has grown into a business partnership that was created in 2019.

This book is particularly special and personal to me because for a long time my relationship with God was hindered by secrets hidden beyond the pews. You see, I myself was a product of one of those secrets.

Throughout the pages of this book, the apostle takes her time to peel back the layers of hurt and disappointment that have pushed so many away from the church, revealing her own hurt and pain. It is designed to help others just like she's helped me.

Reading this book may stir up some feelings inside of you that have been buried by shame and guilt. I hope that this book encourages you to rid yourself of the burden that should never have been yours to carry in the first place. I pray that God speaks to you through this book, and I hope it helps to bring healing to those who can embark on this journey with us.

Lady Zipporah Anderson, Daughter

DEDICATION

I dedicate the contents of this book to my Best Friend, Lover, Protector, Provider, and all that and more – Jesus Christ! Lord, I present every word back to You as You have given them to me. I give You back this ministry that You gave to me. I love you, Lord, and I thank You for opening the eyes of my understanding so that I would know the hope of my calling. I have to declare that I am nothing without You. I give You all the honor, glory, and praise for helping me with this truth.

Your Baby Girl,

Rain

Praise the Lord! This dedication extends to all my girls and family in the body of Christ. By God's grace and mercy, He has anointed me to release this truth to His body (Daddy's girls).

The Bible tells us that in all of our getting, we must obtain understanding. In obtaining understanding, we must be careful how we hear truth. Luke 8:17, 18: *"For there is nothing hidden that shall not become evident, nor anything secret that will not be known and come out into the open. So be careful how you listen: for whoever has (a teachable heart), to him more (understanding) will be given, and whoever does not have (a longing for truth) even what he thinks he has will be taken away from him."* Based on this passage of scripture, there is a way to listen.

In listening to the Word of God, we can obtain understanding in spiritual things or lose what we have received through the Word of God to the mind of the flesh. So, I cover your minds as you read, and I plead the blood of Jesus over you now! My prayer is that you have an ear to hear correctly what God is saying to His body (especially Daddy's little girls), in the area of healing, deliverance, and spiritual warfare. You cannot read this book with the mind of the flesh. The carnal mind cannot submit to that of the spirit. I want the Lord to turn on the spiritual switch inside of you.

Guilt and shame from sexual sins are among the all-time, best-selling weapons that Satan uses against countless people in the church, as well as in the world. These sexual sins are not always the act, but the desire. For example, having a roaming eye. With many cell phones you may come into an area that can incur roaming charges. When that happens, it's up to you to make the decision whether you want to pay for the roaming charges. So it is with fantasy. It can be just as dangerous as the act. So, know that your suffering is only to take you closer to God, not further away.

INTRODUCTION

God allowed me to be the founder of The Wailing Wall Prayer Ministry. It is a deliverance ministry in which we believe in casting the devil out!!! But the one thing I want you to know is that you can't get delivered until you acknowledge that you have a problem. This ministry that God birthed in me was born out of pain, joy, weaknesses, strengths, sadness, happiness, mountain-top, and valley experiences. The things I went through taught me how to pray, and not only to pray, but to pray until I got through to God, beyond the first and second heaven activity, where the prince of the power of the air resides. Quite simply, this means not being detoured or distracted by those things that hinder our prayer lives, especially when we have an urgent request to present to God.

I am well acquainted with sex, church, and true-life secrets beyond the pews. As you read this book, you will find that there are so many women, men, boys, and girls, across every ethnic background and culture, who can relate to this message. Many of them have played tug-of-war between the desire of what they have experienced in the world and being saved and godly in the church. Many times, our lives can become a mixture of religion, sex, love, and failure. Failure because we not only let ourselves down, but God as well.

Is it alright if I just focus on my girls first and foremost? Various times, in these situations, if we're not very careful, we will fall into religious etiquette – knowing how to do what needs to be done for a favorable appearance to our peers. We fail to realize and recognize the man who really loves us unconditionally is Jesus.

Secrets Beyond the Pews ... Shhh! is a voice for that little girl who has been turned out by the pastor who just happened to be a woman who liked young girls. It has caused her to leave the church and live a lifestyle of lesbianism. And it has left her thinking that no one is saved. Or what about the little boy whose mother was the missionary or the evangelist or a preacher who was so caught up in church that her son didn't feel comfortable telling her that the choir director was molesting him. Now he's living a life of promiscuity with perversion, pornography, hidden lust, and masturbation, with women in the light, but secretly desiring boys in the dark.

Yes, these are secrets beyond the pews! This book is your voice! I'm talking about the kind of secrets that you have been afraid to tell anyone for fear (false evidence appearing real) of what the results may be with your congregations, members, and friends; fear that you will no longer be accepted in your families because now you're different, broken, and, believe it or not, looking for love in all the wrong places.

This book is your voice. Listen, if you don't deal with IT (sin beyond the pews – secrets), you can never get the healing and wholeness that you so desperately deserve. Listen to my heart, my sisters and brothers. If you don't deal with the issues of your hearts, your children will face these same demons. (Ezekiel 18:2 talks about the sins of the fathers.) So now it becomes a generational curse that comes into your family lineage.

In most churches, from the pulpit to the pew, we only hear about how we/they categorize sin, making one sin better or less than the other. For example, lying is not as bad as fornication. Having sex outside of marriage is not as bad as being a member of the LGBT community. But believe when I say that one sin is no worse than the other. All sin stinks in the nostrils of God.

You see, in the world, Egypt, or in Pharaoh's house, we knew and were used to players playing the games of love, sex, and infatuation. Didn't you know that we were players too? So, we not only played, but we also continued to enter into a oneness with thieves, liars, haters, and abusers. Do you get the picture?

In no wise when you come into the house of God do you look for these worldly spirits and traits of your once-known abuser to follow you into the church. It's hard to discern the red flags that are constantly showing up before your face. You become jealous and possessive of what's not yours. The bad tempers, acts of cruelty, verbal abuse of your looks and character tear you down mentally and emotionally, taking away your self-worth. And let's not forget those controlling spirits. Remember, reader, deliverance starts with acceptance that there is a problem. So, get your mind freed. This book is your voice! Now open up your mouth and speak!

I want to pray this prayer over you before we go any further. Father God, bless the reader of this book. I bind every evil demonic detraction that would take their mind into different directions as they read and digest what You're saying to our spirit man. We know that Your Word has spoken that the carnal mind cannot perceive spiritual things for they are spiritly discerned. So, Father, in the name of Jesus Christ, open our spiritual ears that we may hear what the spirit is saying to the church. Enlighten the eyes of our understanding for Your Word says, *"In all of thy getting get an understanding."*

So, Father God, we implore You to cover us with Your blood and allow us to go deeper in Your spirit as we

Chapter 1

PERVERSE ILLUSIONS

Everyone has a story. In order to explain my story better I will share a few excerpts from my book, *From Satan To God,* here and from time to time, to go a little deeper for you to understand what I'm talking about. In my book, there's a chapter titled, "I've Fallen, and I Can't Get Up." Sound familiar?

Most of all, I was a fallen woman. I was a secret lover. A certain man had me going in circles like a dog chasing his own tail. There are many veils of illusion and fantasies in all of our lives. There's a magical fascination of what the dark side of sin and lust are – affairs in which you can feel passion and obsession all at the same time. I said in my blog, "If I (whoever you may be) only had a brain, things would be different. I had a heart full of love, and courage to engage, but my mind..."

Most of the time we find ourselves dealing with resistance we can't explain. Many times, there are hidden spirits of which we are not aware, that may be lying dormant until a trigger comes along. These perverse spirits may be why you can't get delivered and set free from the spirit of LUST, and because it's a four-letter word as well, we can easily confuse it with LOVE. You cannot beat the devil at his own game. You have a part to do as well. See, a lot of people underestimate the power of these spirits, and therefore do not know how to first of all, recognize them. If a person takes a venomous snake home, pets it and calls it his or her pet, and the creature bites him and he dies, thinking it was trustworthy, then he or she is considered foolish and unlearned. These are powerful spirits and should be dealt with as such, with and through the power of the living God.

So, now let's talk a bit about relationships and love. I want to share with you the relationship that should have been the breaking point in my life. This one cut me to the core because it was different from all the rest. Why? Because this one was founded in the church.

Some would have even said I was anointed to sing a little bit, preach, and pray. But they forgot that gifts and callings of God were without repentance (see Romans 11:29). My title and anointing didn't stop me from making wrong choices.

Now I know some of you would say I was so naïve to get myself entangled into this one. First off, I'm proud to say that I got saved in August of 1979 (probably my 1st mistake; pride goeth before a fall). There wasn't any holiness doctrine being taught by the preacher in the

Baptist church I came up in. There was no deliverance...from anything. So that meant, no demons being cast out. During that era, a popular song was, "It's Your Thing." It encouraged people to do whatever they wanted to do. Hmmm, think about it. No guidance.

The Bible says in Psalms 81:12, "So I gave them over to their stubborn hearts, to live by their own plans." Do anything, say anything, just say, "Lord, forgive me!" You didn't have to change, but remained the same...in the same lifestyle, because Jesus loves me, and He does but...You can stay, or should I say continue to live a sinful life and you're going to heaven anyway.

Have you ever noticed that EVERYBODY goes to heaven? You know they were as mean as rattle snakes and NEVER REPENTED, and they get to go to heaven to be in a better place? Jesus! Well, if that were the case none of us would have to change nor be converted from a lifestyle of sin.

And Then There's This

One evening I discovered my two young daughters sitting on the outside steps, talking about me in a very negative way. There was always somebody talking about me. My granny, (Mama Dear or to some Mud-dear) use to tell me, "Rain, people are always going to talk about you, whether you doing good or bad. But the time to worry is when they're not talking about you at all." She would say it quite often.

My mother taught me how to pray at an early age, which I always have done, drunk or sober. So, after coming in and going into my little prayer room (the bathroom), I realized that I was dealing with demonic spirits and activities that I couldn't explain at the time.

Many toxic relationship habits are baked into our culture, and we end up accepting them as normal. This is exactly what I did. It was okay that he and I went to the same church, right? I couldn't marry someone else's husband, could I? Yet here I was, in my stinking thinking...Love makes it right. I was trying to bring comfort to this man of God after his mother had passed. Out of all the people who were a significant part of his life, along with his wife and children, he came by my house and sit in quietness with me and my children. I felt bewildered but honored at the same time.

He wanted to get away from everyone else and I was his scapegoat. My heart went out to him because my own mother had passed just a few years prior.

After a while, he wanted me to ride to the mortuary with him to go and view his mother's body for the first time since she had passed. I stood by him, not knowing what to say or what to do. He was always this tower of strength to everyone, so it was touching to see him in this very vulnerable state as he looked upon her lifeless body lying there. Even though he said nothing to me, he managed to stop on the way out for a few words to those who were coming in to view her body, and to share their condolences. Really, I only wanted to be saved and comforting as I watched him hold all of that hurt and pain inside, knowing he was an only child.

We rode around for a bit after we had left the mortuary, and then we stopped on some corner in Pasadena. I don't even remember the street exactly. While we sat there and talked, he asked me so softly and gently, "Can I kiss you?" Why I didn't say no, I don't know to this day. But I didn't. Come on. I had come out of the world, and I wasn't trying to let the world back in but... I consented and told him that he could. Right then I felt the exchange of spirits, his to mine. I didn't know it, but I would soon fall in love with my capturer.

That started a very different roller coaster ride. He and I started spending more and more time together in and out of the church. He was so different from any of the other men that I had been involved with in my lifetime. There was nothing that I asked for or wanted that he did not provide for me and my family. Welcome to the dark side, Lorraine.

Let me talk for a moment to daddy's little girls. Be careful when men start to give you things. What woman or little girl doesn't like/love beautiful things, especially if you've never had them before. Mama used to tell us as young girls, when men just start giving you things, money, etc., usually, they want something in return.

Think about motive. What was the motive behind his sudden interest? Think, do I have my high beams on or am I just being giddy (stuck on stupid)? How many know that you can get stuck like a truck in the mud going nowhere fast? Our prayer *should* be, "Lord let me see the real! Quicken me to see the heart." Girls, don't be a hamburger chick. Oh, he brought me a hamburger; he loves me. I'm going to give him ALL of my good and plenty. Stop, put your thinking caps on. Is he buying other booties (aka HAMBURGERS) beside mine?

Meanwhile, I was getting everything that I wanted. It was drawing me in tighter and tighter, and closer and closer, until I was trapped. Right didn't matter anymore. I couldn't break loose on my own.

Quite a while had passed, and I finally discussed my situation with a couple of people in SECRET. They told me the truth, that the man I was so involved with was never going to marry me. To add salt to the injury, prophets and prophetesses continued to come in and release the word in the atmosphere of the church saying, "No one up in here is going to marry THIS MAN."

In my mind I'm holding on because I know as close as we are he's going to do right by me...Right? He promised. We are in the church.

See, in the world I was known as Candy Love. The Candy was not only good, but it was great. The song by Mr. Z.Z. Hill, "Love is So Good When You're Stealing It," was our song. Get the picture?

Back at the ranch, rather than be true to his word, he chose to keep on stealing it in SECRET. Well, not exactly stealing, but you know what I mean.

I continued to wear my long, long, dresses. No make-up, no extra fingernails or fingernail polish, no colored hair, no pants, none of it. It wasn't after hours, but it was after church. He would say, "Let's go get something to eat." Smooth right? Well, it was smooth if you weren't looking. You remember the old saying, "Oops upside your head?" It was oops that long dress I was tripping on, up over my head.

I wanted to get married; I can't lie. The sex kept getting gooder and gooder to me. I know, the language isn't exactly the most proper. I wanted to pull away for many

Perverse Illusions

years and many times, but girls, it's hard to stop doing something when it's good to you and the flesh is live and in control.

Chapter 2

SINS OF THE FLESH

The Bible says in 1 Corinthians 6:9-20, *"Do you not know that the unrighteous will not inherit or have any share in the kingdom of God? Do not be deceived; neither the sexually immoral, nor idolaters, nor adulterers, nor effeminate (by perversion), nor those who participate in homosexuality, nor thieves, nor the greedy, nor drunkards, nor revilers (whose words are used as weapons to abuse, insult, humiliate, intimidate, or slander), nor swindlers will inherit or have any share in the kingdom of God. And such were some of you (before you believed), you were sanctified (set apart for God, and made holy), you were justified (declared free of guilt) in the name of the Lord Jesus Christ and in the (Holy) Spirit of our God (the source of the believer's new life and changed behavior). Everything is permissible for me, but not all things are beneficial. Everything is permissible for me, but I will not be enslaved by anything (and brought under its power, allowing it to control me). Food is for the stomach and the stomach for food, but God will do away with both of them. The body is not intended for sexual immorality, but for the Lord, and the Lord is for the body*

9

(to save, sanctify, and raise it again because of the sacrifice of the cross). And God has not only raised the Lord (to life) but will also raise us up by His power. Do you not know that your bodies are members of Christ? Am I therefore to take the members of Christ and make them part of a prostitute? Certainly not! Do you not know that the one who joins himself to a prostitute is one body with her? For He says, 'The two shall be one flesh' But the one who is united and joined to the Lord is one spirit with Him. Run away from sexual immorality (in any form, whether thought or behavior, whether visual or written). Every other sin that a man/woman commits is outside the body, but the one who is sexually immoral sins against his own body. Do you not know that your body is a temple of the Holy Spirit who is within you, whom you have (received as a gift) from God, and that you are not your own (property)? You were bought with a price (you were actually purchased with the precious blood of Jesus and made His own). So then, honor and glorify God with your body."

There is a spirit of shame that comes with the spirit of lust, pornography, masturbation, fornication, adultery, homosexuality lesbianism, prostitution, chronic dissatisfaction, excessive appetite, swingers, phone sex, etc.

All of these things can keep you in bondage, guilt, and shame.

These are some of the sins that a lot of people in church don't really want to confess because of fear that they will be judged and stoned right on the spot. The spirit of shame is a master demon. Shame runs with a seducing spirit. It's a drawing and alluring spirit. It will always pull you in a negative direction. The power force behind these spirits is very strong. It's like opening a can of worms that you cannot close back without the help of the Lord. Many times, we can recognize pornography, lust, masturbation, but we cannot recognize the strongman behind it. These are seducing spirits, alluring, mind binding spirits that witches and warlocks use to keep you in hard core bondage. My brother, Timothy, said in his book, 1 Timothy 4:1: *"Now the spirit speaketh expressly, that in the latter times some shall depart from the faith, giving heed to seducing spirits, and doctrines of devils."* My brother Peter said it like this: *"Knowing this first: that scoffers, mockers will come in the last days, walking according to their own lusts"* (2 Peter 3:3).

So, when these spirits are in charge, they are hard to resist, but the Word of the Lord tells us, *"Resist the devil and he will* (that's a promise) *flee from you"* (see James

Sins of the Flesh

4:7). That first part of this scripture says, *"Submit yourselves, then, to God."*

Chapter 3

MY SALVATION

In 1979, long before the toxic relationship I described in Chapter 1 occurred, something happened to me that would change my life forever. God sent an unsaved woman to me with a gift of prophecy to tell me about a change that God would bring into my life shortly thereafter. This woman was a cousin of mine who came to me one day in the month of August. She said she'd had a dream concerning me the night before. She had seen me saved, not drinking alcohol or doing drugs, partying, fornicating, etc.

While she was bringing me this message, I was high. Now, I believed the word that she had said, and I stated to her, "I wish I was saved right now." We laughed about it and went on our way. But because of the lifestyle that I was living I felt that I needed to be baptized again, as I had been previously. I knew that this was a means of all of my sins being washed away, and I so desperately needed the change.

During this time, I was always praying to the Lord and singing gospel songs on my own, even though I was still getting high on drugs such as PCP, alcohol, cocaine, pills, (red devils, yellow jackets, black mollies, and mini bennies), and also men. Yes, I was addicted to men, and in some ways I still am. Only this time it's in a Godly way (smile). These were simple, but honest prayers and songs that had been taught to me by my mother. You may ask me why I would pray in my condition? The answer is that I really didn't know why, but to say that it was already in me to do so.

On a Friday afternoon sometime in early August, I was walking back home from working for one of my aunts who lived not too far from where we were staying in the city of Lynwood, California, on Alpine Street. I never will forget that place. As I had gotten to where we were living I happened to walk up on my two older daughters who were sitting at the bottom of the steps of our small apartment building. As I got closer to them I could hear them talking. As I looked at them, I was so proud to be their mother; glad to see them after a hard day's work. When I reached the place where they were sitting, to my amazement, those Negros were talking about me...again! Bad!

That would not have been so bad if what they were saying was something nice. But I could hear them talking before they realized that I was there, like two grown people, saying, "Dog, mama just be wanting to get high all the time." "She don't care anything about us." Even though what they were saying was half true, I always cared, wow! When I heard those words they were like a sharp knife piercing my very soul. What they didn't understand was that they were my LIFE! Now, if you loved your children the way that I loved mine and had poured yourself into your children like I had, because their no-good daddies had left me carrying the bag (after the fun was over, they were over and they just wanted to play house with no commitments), that would have broken your heart too, to hear what they were saying, as it did mine. I had to realize that they were only repeating what they had heard others say, they didn't really know. These girls were only eight and 10 years old. (These children are still my life today along with all the rest of them that God has given me since then.)

I spoke to them and said, "Other people can talk about me all day, and say whatever they like, but when you two talk about me that is what hurts me the most...you two." I then sent them into the house with a loud hurting voice as though I was about to cry. I followed them but went into another room and sat down and began to talk to the Lord again.

I hear the word of the Lord for somebody who's reading my story right now, which says, *"The Lord is nigh unto them that are of a broken heart: and saveth such as be of a contrite spirit"* (Psalm 34:18). The Message Bible reads like this: *"If your heart is broken, you'll find God right there; if you're kicked in the gut, he'll help you catch your breath."* Psalm 51:16, 17 says, *"Going through the motions doesn't please you; a flawless performance is nothing to you. I learned God-Worship when my pride was shattered. Heart-shattered lives ready for love don't for a moment escape God's notice."*

God Does Talk to Sinners

I continued to talk to the Lord in my despair. People have said down through the years that the Lord doesn't hear or speak to sinners, but I beg to differ with them because the Bible says that while Paul, before he became the apostle, was on his way to imprison and kill more of the Jews (Christians), the Lord met him on the Damascus Road and knocked him off his beast and blinded him by a great light and spoke to him, asking him, "Paul, why do you persecute me?" Now here's my point: Paul answered and said back to the Lord, "Lord, who art thou?" So that lets me know that Jesus can and will speak to whomever He will, and we can hear Him in whatever state we're in.

I heard the Lord for the first time speak to me in my heart. Yes, the Lord was now speaking back to ME. This was my own Damascus Road experience. The Lord said to me, "O foolish Galatian, who has bewitched thee whose eyes have been evidently set toward me that you should not obey the truth?" I didn't even know that this scripture was in the Bible at the time! I thought I was really crazy, and everyone else did too. But I knew that I had heard His voice. I thought to myself, am I bewitched? I had heard the words witchcraft and superstition most all of my life. But the only bewitched that I knew personally was on television with the name of Samantha who starred in the tv sitcom.

I continued to meditate on those words as much as I could under the circumstances, since I was still staying as high as I could. My prayer room and getaway place even as it is to this day, was my bathroom. So that's where I went and began to pray and sing an old Shirley Caesar song entitled "Put Your Hand in the Hand of the Man That Stilled the Waters." The Lord knew how much I needed my waters to be stilled, and the sea of my emotions to be at peace.

Anyway, as it was getting close to time for the scheduled baptism that I so desired, which the pastor whom I was under at the time had agreed to... Wait; let me back up a little and put this in reverse. I was still smoking my reefer, PCP, cocaine, and having a nicotine fit regularly. I knew that all of these things and habits were not good for me, but I kept on doing those things faithfully. I even read the warning label on every package of cigarettes I bought. I went as far as buying them and then throwing them away in somebody else's trashcan, but before the day was gone, I would be going back to find them again, just like the dog returning back to his vomit. I felt I needed to get one more drag, obeying that nicotine demon. Can you believe that? Being hooked on a piece of paper and some tobacco, puff after puff, one right after another and then another. All of those spirits that had found suitable housing in me were demanding obedience from me all at the same time.

So, I remained in a state of confusion, darkness, and obscurity. I found myself like the man in the Bible living in the country of the Gadarenes who had a spirit in him called Legion. This man lived in tombs, a place for the dead. This was a place of interment or a grave. But when this crazy madman who could not be bound with chains saw Jesus from afar off, with just a look, the spirit ran and worshiped Him and then it cried out (see Mark 5:6). People had tried to bind him with fetters at the feet as well, and he would often pluck asunder the fetter into pieces: neither could they tame him. Yet he ran to Jesus and the spirit cried out of the man, the Bible says, with a loud voice saying, "What have we to do with you Jesus, Son of the Most-High? Swear to God that you won't torture me!" Jesus asked him, "What is your name?" The demon replied, "Legion, for we are many." This was the demon talking. Jesus said, "Come out of this man, you evil spirit." Because of the authority Jesus had, the spirit departed from him. If I didn't have Legion, then I had all of his other relatives living in me, and there was no one around me at this time in my life who knew how to operate in the authority needed to set me free.

During this period in my life, it may have been sometime during the early part of summer, or late fall season, I was still looking for answers. Usually, around this time my skin would peel very badly (due to climate changes, some people do in certain seasons, especially in their hands, feet, lips, and also around their noses). At this particular time, I had started pulling off the dead skin, but right in the arch of my foot I had peeled it until it was very painful. It became physically excruciating and sensitive until it felt like it was an open wound with which I was suffering. I could hardly tolerate the pain. I couldn't even put on my shoe due to the pain. It had come up in my arch all of a sudden. The pain kept increasing, getting greater and greater, seemingly with every minute.

On this particular night some of our friends and I were all in one of my sister's rooms, hanging out and listening to some misty blues with the likes of some of the popular artists of the current time, Tyrone Davis, Teddy Pendergrass, BB King, Bobby Bland, Stephanie Mills, Peabo Bryson, Aretha Franklin, etc. All the while we were still getting high on our drugs and alcohol. It had started getting late, so everybody just started dropping off to sleep right where they were. As I was lying in my spot the pain began to remind me that it was not leaving. I began to moan and rub my feet. Believe it or not I began to pray and say to God, "Lord, if this pain is coming from you, could you please lift it right now, please." Speaking in a loud whisper, I said to the Lord, "Lord if you are allowing me to go through what I'm going through then please give me a sign." I didn't believe that God would really give me a sign, but He did.

When Gideon wasn't sure that the Lord was calling him to be His warrior, the Lord gave him a sign with the option of the fleece before he himself knew that the Lord was with him (see Judges 6:37-39).

So now I'm praying, really seeking Him. And remember, the sign came as the pain in my feet. The pain was continual, so I groaned and whispered again, "Okay Lord, please ease this pain." Believe it or not the pain mysteriously started to lift. I looked down and fell asleep.

When I got up the next morning I was like an old refrigerator; I could hardly keep it to myself, but I did. With all that was going on at the house I don't think that the Lord wanted me to say all that was taking place, nor did He want me to tell them what had happened because He knew how they would react. But when doing drugs is your lifestyle, and you're getting as high as your money allows, it's hard to keep such important things to yourself. Also, He knew how hard it would be for them to think that I was telling them the truth. There is a scripture which says, *"The carnal mind cannot perceive spiritual things"* (Romans 8:7).

It's getting closer to baptism day. It was another night in which friends had gathered all day and all night. Some of them who were girls, went as far as wearing men's clothing. They were cross-dressers.

Some of the women would make sure that their hair was cut like that of a man. I felt that this was going on because the devil knows that a women's hair is her glory; and of course, the men would do the opposite. They were running as it were, in and out of our house, going out to get and to bring in more and more drugs. It seemed like they always brought in with them strong demonic forces. The devil made it seem like we were the people to know and to hang out with.

There is a quote made popular by various individuals which says, "Everyone sees who I appear to be, but only a few know the real me." The women looked like men, acted like men, although you could look at them and tell that they were actually women, just like you can today.

Help Me Lord, I Need Peace

Now it's getting even closer to the baptism day. I'm at the house, so confused with demons and demonic activity going on that I felt I had to get away...quickly. Somewhere, anywhere, I could find some peace! But I didn't know where I could go. Every room that I went into was already occupied. So, in haste I turned and grabbed my Bible. Holding it tightly to my chest, I almost ran out of the house, trying to find a place of peace and rest. I just wanted to sit down so that I could read.

There were many times on my "drug trips" when my mind would leave me (literally). I would find a sense of peace and calmness in the words of that book, the Bible. There were times when I would walk. It seemed like I would be always looking for my mother, no matter what the distance. On those trips it seemed like once in my mother's presence, there was peace for my tormented soul.

My mother would know that I was high, drunk, in an out-of-it state of mind, and she would sit me down by her feet. This reminded me of Mary who chose to sit at the feet of Jesus. Mother would put her hand on my back as if to say, "Peace be still, my child." She would then turn on a gospel radio station. Even as she did then and I do now, she was always listening to some preacher on the air. Thank

God for those preachers... the Lord knew we needed His Word and maybe He had let mother in on it.

Once I heard the Word, not just the voice of a man or a woman, but the living Word of God through His powerful anointing, the sound of the Word made my whole body, soul, and spirit calm down (faith cometh by hearing).

Well, back at the ranch. I was still looking for a peaceful place to sit down so that I could read a Word (the Bible) when finally, I left the house and began to walk the streets of Lynwood, walking away from the house weeping, and talking to Jesus.

I did not know how long I had walked until I saw the park that was located on Rosecrans Blvd. Here is the bizarre thing: as I walked I saw what looked like benches, and lights around the park. Since it was already nightfall, it looked like those lights were electrical. As I began to walk toward the lights that I saw, I happened to look down, and right by my left foot I saw what looked like an electrical snake. At the moment I didn't ask any questions. I just looked up to heaven and took off running, screaming, yelling, and crying in the loudest voice that I could, "JESUS DON'T LEAVE ME DOWN HERE!!!" All the while I was running, I never looked down again. I didn't know if the snake was following me or not.

When I was little I used to hear my mother and some of the other older folks talk about why mother didn't want to move back to the country. One of the things that I had heard mother say was that she was walking back home from somewhere, and two blue racer snakes smelled the milk in her breasts and began to chase her. But as my mother, being a fast runner, so I'm told, was approaching the porch, my Grannie saw her running. She grabbed her shotgun and shot both of them as mother ran past her.

While I'm running, still looking up, screaming again to the top of my voice, "JESUS DON'T LEAVE ME DOWN HERE!!!" all of a sudden out of nowhere there appeared two men right in front of me. It seemed as if it happened quicker than lightning. One stood out in front, and the other seemed to be standing on the side of him. It seemed as if they were connected because they were so close. The one who stood to the side, maybe more toward the back of the one in front who did all the talking, never said anything to me, but stood quietly watching, not being distracted by anything that was going on around us.

Now the front man began to call me, saying, "Hey, are you all right?" When I noticed that they were there, I was startled again. I was still frightened and greatly alarmed by their presence. The man who stood in the front of the other man began to speak to me again and this time he was reaching out his hand. I looked at his hand but was so afraid that I pulled my hand back further from his so that he could not touch me. He then asked me, "What is your name?" I should have said Legion, but still with great fear, I didn't answer. However, his voice was so peaceful that I begin to calm down. Finally, I said to him, "My name is Lorraine." He then said, "Lorraine, we saw you running and crying out to Jesus, and we ran over to stop you because you were headed right into the middle of Rosecrans." Rosecrans Blvd was always busy, seemingly day and night. But it was just them and me there that I could see.

Standing there in the dark of the night, I began to explain that the very next day I was going to be baptized, and that there was so much going on at my house that I couldn't find any place to read my Bible and that I had no peace. I also told them that when I had reached the park I had seen what appeared to be lights and benches. I guess I was still talking kinda fast because of how afraid I was. I went on to say that when I had begun to walk over to the light is when I looked down and saw the snake at my feet. The man who did all of the talking then said to me, "Lorraine, that was the devil, and he was trying to kill you before you went into the water on tomorrow."

My Salvation

By this time, I had calmed down enough to ask the man, "Who are you?" Notice that I didn't say the men because they seemed as though they were one person. The spokesman of the two said, "My name is Michael." He then asked me, "Are you alright now?" And I replied, "Yes." As I began to walk away, I thought of how great the peace was that surrounded me at the time with these two men. It was so different from all other men I'd had encounters with...It was such great peace...unspeakable peace. I also thought to myself, did God send His warring angel, Michael, for me? Ummm. I walked home pondering these things in my mind and in my heart, remembering how they (angels?) were right there, manifested to save my life before this seemingly long journey of deliverance and holiness began.

Chapter 4

THE NIGHT BEFORE

The night before the actual baptism, the spirit of fear came upon me like I had never known it before. I was so fearful of going into that water. I recalled a time when my two older children had cut the fool, as the old folks would say, about having to be baptized. I was in my early twenties around this time, and I knew that this was what we did in our faith because the preachers and my mama said so. That was all the understanding that you needed, no questions asked. So, when the time came for these girls to get into the water they kicked and screamed so much and so loud that the preachers sent them back home in a hurry. I had not gone that particular Sunday, for whatever the reason. I can't recall it right now (may have had a hangover or something) but I didn't go. When the people told me how they had acted I couldn't be angry with them. The Bible says that faith cometh by hearing. So, what I did was I started playing one of my old songs by the legendary Williams Brothers, "Tis the Old Ship of Zion." After a few days of playing and singing that song, my children came to me and said, "Mommy, we want to be baptized now.

The Night Before

I relate that incident because at this particular time of my second baptism, that spirit of fear came in upon me so strongly about going into the water the next day that I could hardly contain myself. Howbeit, no one knew what was going on with me because no one believed that there was a real transformation going on in me. But, as it was my usual practice to go into my bathroom to sing and to pray, this night I got into the tub on my knees. I seemingly went into some kind of trance state of mind. I knew that I was in the presence of the living God just like I was a little child. At this point it seemed like a hand came through my hand and began to turn on the cold water while my head was bowed down in submissiveness.

I was still somewhat frightened, but I knew that I was not in control. I didn't know it then, but I know today that it was the Holy Spirit that was at work again, even as He had moved on the face of the deep when the earth was void and without form. The Spirit of the Lord was moving in that bathroom for little old me. As the tub continued to fill up with cold water, I looked up toward the roof of our apartment, and it seemed as though the roof opened and there were human-like figures, but you could tell that they were people. It seemed as though these people were sitting around the top of the roof, but they seemed to be sitting in the clouds. Do some of you remember as little children we would look up into the sky and try to figure out the images that were there? Well, this night was like that. I didn't know who they were, nor could I figure out all of their faces, but I just knew that they were there. When the tub had reached its peak, that same hand came back through my hand and turned the water off. As I was still on my knees, it seemed like someone took my head as if I was being baptized in that cold water and baptized me right there. I know that this may sound far-fetched to many of you. But it literally happened just like I'm telling you.

After that, all of the fear that was once there was totally gone. Hallelujah! I didn't know it then, but all of the demons that I had housed in my body were being tormented at the very presence of God! My sisters and my brothers, this is the moment that fear left me!

The Night Before

Chapter 5

THE NEXT DAY

Now, I am ready for my big day. When it finally came, instead of the spirit of fear there was a spirit of joy and expectation. When we arrived at the church, I remember being put in a room to wait for my turn. They wrapped me up in a white sheet. As I sat there in that room my cousin who had brought me the word prior (the prophecy) came into the room where I was. She said, "Rain, in that dream I saw myself anointing your feet with some anointed oil. I sent for some from off of the television." She then proceeded to anoint my feet. While she did that, I had my Bible and it was like something spoke to me (I say "something" because I was not familiar with saying the Holy Ghost or the Holy Spirit) to read Matthew 6:1, which says, *"Take heed that you do not your chartable deeds before men to be seen by them. Otherwise, you have no reward from your Father in heaven."*

By that time, they were ready for me. I remembered when I walked forward, in the vision that my cousin had seen, there was also the order in which we were supposed to have gone into the water. We were trying hard to follow the instructions of the dream since everything else was coming together so quickly. This is no reflection on my sister or on my cousin, but as I'm writing this I'm reminded of Jesus hanging between the two thieves because my sister went first and then myself, and finally my cousin, who also wanted to get baptized. I remember just before my pastor took me down into the water he spoke these words: "...and some will even preach the gospel."

This was the same man I had gone to earlier and told him I thought God was calling me to preach and he had laughed and laughed and laughed at me in unbelief that the Lord would consider me. "In the name of the Father, in the name of the Son, in the name of the Holy Ghost," and I was emerged into that cold, chilly water, coming up this time changed. I still didn't understand that God was at work in my life then and there, but I felt a change. One of the mothers of that day broke out with an old Dr. Watt's hymn, about the Lord having another witness. And it was true...He did have another witness!

Deliverance didn't come right away for me because those whom I was under did not operate in deliverance. So as the journey continued, I was on my way to a new lifestyle of holiness mapped out by God.

When the baptism was over, and everyone went back home, I looked around for my visible change, but I couldn't see any in myself, my sister, or even in my cousin.

Chapter 6

HOW PRAYER GOT ME OUT

Though I had gotten baptized, there still were many changes that were yet to take place in my life, but praying was still something that I would do. There were so many times the power of prayer got me out!. The one that resonates with me at this moment was when I found myself in my first and last abusive relationship with Mr. Love Man. Oh, how fine I thought he was. In that time, just like now, thin was in, so were tall, light-skinned men and women.

I recall walking into the party late one weekend with some family and friends. Looking around the room to see how the party was jumping, my eyes fell on the tall, slender guy standing in the kitchen doorway with his brim tilted. Just as I noticed him, it was for certain that he noticed me also. I thought I just had it like that. Anyway, it didn't seem like there was any other female who was latched on to him that I could see. Somehow during the night, we met and exchanged information. Of course, he said all the right things. Soon after that night, we made plans to meet again and again, until finally I thought it was safe to introduce him to friends and family... even to my children, my two baby girls. This Negro was smoother than butter and slicker than oil. Not one of us detected the real demons on the inside of him until...

One of my cousins and I were hanging out, doing what we did. We got a phone call telling us that her 10-month-old baby had died. We weren't that far away from the house (her brother's house) where she had left the baby. We ran to the house, eyes still foggy and red from the alcohol and weed we had consumed. I believe if my cousin were still living, she would say it's alright to tell this part of the story. Oh, how I loved that little girl; Shikiya Naima was her name. After it was determined that she died from crib death and that there was no foul play, we put her away and believe it or not, we continued with our life of destruction, spiraling down the wrong road.

Shortly after that I came down with what I thought at first was the flu. However, I found out later it was morning sickness. I was pregnant with my third child by my new "him." Third baby's daddy. When I realized that it wasn't the alcohol or the reefer that afternoon that had my head in the toilet, I turned and looked into the eyes of my cousin Brenda Gayle and said to her, "I can't have another baby. I'm only 22 with two babies already. I can't afford another one." In reply to my words, she said, "But Rain, this will be the baby that God is giving us for the one He took. Please have this baby for me and if it's a girl we'll name her Shikiya Naima in remembrance of my baby." I said, "Okay, 'cuz; this will be our baby."

Now walk with me down the corridors of time and see the picture that I'm about to paint for you. When I told this tall bright skinned man that I was carrying his child, oh the joy that he portrayed as he laid across the bed, waiting for me to join him in another night of sexual bliss. It appeared everything was falling into place for me for the first time. But there was this one particular time when he came over to my apartment and the slow jams were playing and the red lights were on and of course it wouldn't be a right night without the drugs. While we sat and talked and kissed, he began to whisper sweet nothings into my ear, "Why should we keep living in two different places when we can move in together, put our monies together, so we can help one another more, Baby." In that moment I really wasn't thinking clearly... I said yes, of course.

Hold on! The Bible says to be sober, be vigilant for your adversary goeth about as a roaring lion SEEKING whom he may devour. That was one of the worst mistakes I'd ever made in my life! Somebody once said it's easy to get into it, but it's hell to get out. For the next three and a half years that's exactly what I went through... HELL! After he had moved in, about maybe a month later I saw the monster he really was, the real person came forth. You see, I had met his representative first. The counterfeit person he didn't want me to see, the abuser...

I turned around one day after having said something that didn't tickle his fancy and there was a hard slap to my face. I literally saw lights and stars. Now even though I had learned to fight to survive, I had never had a boyfriend to ever treat me in such a way. My initial response was that of shock. I couldn't believe that this abuser was in, not out, but in, MY house! I had seen this spirit before, coming up as a little girl, when my dad would fight my mom. The difference between me and my mom is that she was a country girl who was raised with nine boys. She knew how to handle herself quite well. That didn't stop my father from trying to break her to his will. Being traumatized by the constant cursing and fighting, I never thought it would follow me into my young adulthood.

Of course, I told my dad what had happened and waited for him to run up on daddy, a man, but he never made a move on him the way he had me and other girls. It stopped for a moment because of the warning from dad, but when he saw that I only had company every now and then, the abuser showed up again after the baby was born. This time the beating was much more severe. I would wake up with black eyes and my face swollen. He would leave for a while to hang out with his friends and come back with those very famous words: "Baby, I'm so sorry. I love you so much. I really didn't mean to hurt you. I hate to see you look like that. That's why I always have to leave. I really love you so much." And listen to this... "I'll never do it again." We would have sex and all things seemed to be well again for a while.

Some may be asking, "Why did you stay in it for so long?" The Bible speaks of soul ties in 1 Corinthians 6:16, being entangled together with a harlot you become one with that spirit. At first (I can't lie to you), he had me frightened to death by choking me out till I literally passed out, each time coming back to myself with him always standing over me, I guess to see if I was still living.

It got so bad that I started meditating on how I could kill this man. I had people who wanted to do it for me, but I said no, I didn't want them to get in trouble for his murder. One of them said to me after they had found out how he had given me a brutal beat down, "Turn your head and you will never have to worry again."

One night I prayed, which I always did even while I was still in sin. I was taught that by my mother, who had raised us in the church to always pray and take the Lord along with you everywhere you go. So, I said tonight is the night. I'm either going to kill him this time or he's going to kill me. This is it! The first prayer that I prayed was simple, "Lord, take care of my children."

This man always kept his .45 pistol by the bed, so after another fight in which I woke up from being choked out...

Pause and let me interject this right here: He was going through so much with the jealousy, thinking that other men wanted me. He thought I was only going to church to meet other men and that there was no God. I didn't know that my precious babies were being tormented and abused by this demon as well. I couldn't see it and they were afraid to tell me. So girls, when you allow the abuse, many times it will trickle down to your children as well.

Are you still walking with me? Okay, good... I sat on my bed, and I asked in the sweetest voice I could muster up, "Can you please go and get me a glass of water?" He said, "Sure." When he walked out of the room I went to pick up the gun and just at that moment, he stuck his head back in the door just to let me know he had taken all of the bullets out of the gun. I know there had to be another way, but what was it? Being at my wits end, I prayed again, "Lord, if you get me out of this one, I promise YOU, I will never go back again!" It was then that the Lord opened the door and made a way of escape for me and my children after just simply talking to God like Hannah did, after being vexed by her adversary Peninnah (see 1 Samuel 1:1-8).

What I'm trying to tell you is that honest sincere prayer from my heart caused my freedom. There is so much more that I could tell you about how prayer got me out of so many situations, but I will pick back up further on in my story. Reverend R. W. Schambach used to say, "You don't have any problems; all you need is faith in God."

I would like to pause here again to say if you're in an abusive relationship, please don't stay in it, making excuses for their behavior. You have options. There is help available. Most of the time there are three phases with signs to look for, according to the Cycle of Violence cited on the following organization's website, Shelter for Help in Emergency, https://www.shelterforhelpinemergency.org

1. Tension-building phase ~ Walking on eggshells. Everything has to be perfect. Always worrying or in fear of what if. Feeling "something" is about to happen.
2. Acute or crisis phase ~ The blow up, worse than before. Threats. Destruction. Fear for your or your child's safety. Drug and/or alcohol abuse.
3. Calm or honeymoon phase ~ The person you fell in love with. Never happen again. I'll get help. I love you.

Meditation Scripture:

Now faith is the substance of things hoped for and the evidence of things not seen (Hebrews 11:1).

Chapter 7

LEARNING ABOUT THE POWER OF PRAYER

In learning about prayer, I always knew that someone somewhere was praying for me, especially my mother, who, I found out, was an awesome prayer warrior herself, while in the church, that is, and maybe outside of it as well. I would watch my mother so closely. Something seemed like it would make me feel funny; not scary, but... Well, at the time I couldn't explain it. But oh, how I desired to be like my mother. When she would sing, to me it was the most beautiful sound you ever wanted to hear. People would get happy and go to shouting all over the church when she sang. They would cry when she would pray. It seemed like something was being broken or loosed that was holding them captive. I learned that it was those kind of prayers that kept me when I was being molested, raped, running the streets, getting into situations in which I knew I should have died. I learned it was my mother's prayers that I was living on.

Before the Lord took my mother home to be with Him, I recall coming home from church one night. By this time, I had gotten good and saved. Some of the saints and I had been out praying and interceding for some of the people who had asked us to come into their homes to pray. Oh, what an honor to see God move in the homes like He would in the churches. No, you don't hear me. I'm talking about the very power I spoke about earlier falling upon the people in those houses. Well, after one of those nights, I came home full of joy for what the Lord had done. Wow, giving God all the glory! I walked into my house and there was my mother sitting on the living room couch with her leg swollen with fever. She had stepped out of my cousin's van and missed the step and her leg had begun to swell instantly. One of my children was in the other room coughing and choking; something else was going on with another one. Immediately the spirit of the Lord spoke to me to get my anointed oil and go to work.

As I anointed my hands, I went over to mother first. I was concerned because she was a diabetic. I went to where my mother was sitting, and I bowed down by her and placed my hands on her leg and began to pray. While praying I could feel the fever coming up from mother's leg into my hands. I then went into the rooms where my children were lying and began to lay my hands on them. The coughing and choking ceased, and there was calm in the house. I went back into my prayer room, which was in the front of the house, and laid down and went to sleep, not thinking about anything else.

The next morning my mother called me to where she was and said, "Look girl, my leg has gone down and there's no more fever." I said in amazement, "Wow mom. It wasn't me; it was God." She said, "I know, girl."

So many amazing things like that happened as the Lord was teaching me the power of prayer. This was during a time when He was also teaching me to trust Him. Many times, we pray but we don't really, really trust that the Lord can do what we're asking Him to do. So, the Lord will put us in situations or circumstances in which we can't do anything else but trust Him, all the while building our faith in Him. We know that the Bible tells us without faith it is not possible to please Him. This faith walk ain't no joke!

I recall living in Los Angeles on 104th street and Wall where I was used to calling for some help from people, boyfriends, etc., when I was in need of assistance. But I heard the voice of the Lord say to me, "Lorraine, I'm your boyfriend, sugga daddy; call Me and trust Me." Now that might have been alright if my circumstances were different... But instead, my rent was paid but my gas and lights were off at the same time.

A lot of this millennial generation don't know crap about things like that because many of them just feel they're entitled. As for my children, I tried but I had to wait on the Lord to send help. Listen, I tried to get a job, but no doors were opening. I believed God, but my babies and I still had to go through. Not many people even knew what we were dealing with except those who were the closest, and they couldn't help.

My oldest daughter said to me one day after church with her head hung down, "Mom, I know you're living right and believing God. Why won't God help us like He's blessing these other people that ain't living nothing and it seem like they're getting all the blessings?" I just had to look into her face and say to her, "Baby girl, the Lord will provide."

Sometimes waiting in God's waiting room can be very discouraging, but you still have to wait. So, still remaining faithful to my God, I waited, having Bible study by kerosene lamps and trying to take baths by warming pots of water on the hot plate to which my Hispanic neighbors had run an extension cord from their house to ours. Talk about embarrassing... However, with all of that I was still able to take in others who needed shelter and the love of God. I never went to church saying listen ya'll, my gas and lights are off, and I can't get a job so what are you going to do about it? Instead, I went to church almost nightly and praised God like a crazy woman, praised God in every service like all was well...waiting.

Finally, after my prayer time one evening, one of the young ladies whom we had prayed for came over to my house and said the Lord told her to come by and do for me whatever I needed. Sometimes the Lord sends someone whom you least expect. I said, "My gas is off, and it is about $300 or $400 to have it turned back on." She said, "Well whatever it is, God told me to do it." I wanted to cry but instead I just shouted for joy. Not only did she have my gas turned back on, but she also blessed me with a small token of love as well. Hallelujah! Waiting on God, learning to trust Him, knowing that He is real and always there even when you can't trace Him, track Him, or feel Him, you just know in your knower that God keeps His promises.

Shortly after that, one of my nephews was taken from my sister who was on drugs and running the streets at the time, and they needed someone to take the baby. My mother begged me, "Please Rain, I don't want to see my grandchildren in the system." Not knowing that God had a plan and that His plan was working all the time, I gave in and said, "Mom, I'll do it, but the gas just got back on, and the lights are still off." I was reminded again that the Lord would make a way. Therefore, I agreed to meet with the workers for her case. My nephew was in bad shape. My sister had left him in the hospital unattended. Of course, it was reported.

Praying and waiting on God, getting a new baby with no lights and no money – impossible. Well, the worker made an appointment to come and check out the house. All of my roommates and other children were sitting outside in the car, right in the front of the house. I wish you could visualize this picture with me. I had a house full of children with mine and my friend's and most of them were stuffed in my station wagon in the front of the house on the street. When the lady came, I opened up all the windows and curtains to let as much light in the house as possible. The worker checked the whole house and finally she asked, "Are you not turning on the lights to save electricity?" I said, "Oh yes ma'am, you're absolutely right." Now remember I'm waiting on the Lord. The woman said to me before she left, "You know, it's a wonderful thing you're doing for your sister and nephew, but did you know that the state will pay you for keeping your nephew?" I said, "No ma'am, I didn't know it, but I wasn't doing it for money." She said, "Someone else would get it, Lorraine, and it could help."

You know that along with the baby came money to pay the light bill and to buy food. I never would have guessed that the Lord was going to bless me with a handsome young man to take care of, and a job all at the same time. Now my new son had to be on this Promo machine (Pulmonary Nebulizer Breathing Machine) two, three, or four times a day. The children and I would take turns putting the medicine in the machine and giving him his treatments. But one evening after church I had him with me in my prayer room and he had an attack and couldn't breathe. I was so exhausted from walking home from church and getting in so late. Everyone else was already sleeping and it was my turn to give the baby his treatment, but I just couldn't get up. So, I prayed and said, "Lord, I can hardly raise my head up." At that moment, I lie to you not, there appeared a giant angel in my prayer room. I couldn't get up, but I could only look up as he picked up my son and it seemed as though he was putting him on his shoulder. But as I laid there, it seemed like the higher he lifted him the more my son had disappeared. I think I may have fallen asleep at that time. I don't know how long it was between me falling to sleep and the angel picking him up, but I remember when he placed the baby back down beside me. There was an indescribable peace that came into the room. The baby was at peace like he hadn't been since before I picked him up from the hospital. After the Angel had picked the baby up and he (the baby) disappeared for I don't know how long. Shortly after that experience my son was healed and never needed that ole Machine again.

Praise God for his supernatural healing power. Hallelujah!

When my son became a teenager, he told me about when he tried out some new drug for the first time, which took him on a bad trip. He said, "Mom, the Lord took me back to that day when the angel came into the room and lifted me up." He said, "Mom, I died that day, and then He showed me a vision of hell. It scared me to death."

Learning to wait and trust in the Lord and lean not to your own understanding is one thing to know, but yet another thing to live and experience. Therefore, at the end of the day as the saying goes...The beat goes on or should I say went on.

For the next three years, everything around me seemed like it was the same, but in essence I was continually changing in the way that I saw things, and of course, those around me. My family and associates knew that there had been a change in Rain that they couldn't describe or understand...BUT GOD!

Romans 12:2: *Do not be conformed to this world, but be transformed by the renewal...*

1 Peter 2:15: *For this is the will of God, that by doing good you should put to silence the ignorance of foolish people.*

Chapter 8

HOW COULD THIS HAPPEN IN THE CHURCH?

I didn't know then how much my life paralleled my mother's. I mentioned in my first book the two main men in the church who had left her wounded, both of whom left her with a baby. One of them was a preacher and the other a deacon. The only difference between my mother and me was the two I had an encounter with were both pastors. Mother left the church backslidden, whereas I stayed in the church still trying to make sense out of it all. I believe that there is a woman, boy, girl, and even a man somewhere in the house of God saying, "Why me? This kind of thing doesn't happen in the church. Help! I've fallen and I can't get up!"

The first pastor I had become involved with – only a one-time slip (before the toxic relationship described in Chapter 1). Notice this: those slips count too – those times when you say to yourself, "This one time won't hurt. Plus, nobody knows. I can stop at any time." But even though it was one time with this pastor, I learned later that he had raped one of my teenage daughters and the other one he had molested. How could anything like that happen on my watch? Any mother in her right mind that could endure such a thing in or out of the church would have lost her natural mind. But I didn't...

The Enemy Really Thought He Had Me

The Lord is really a keeper. I had literally lost my mind before I converted to holiness. The Lord was calling me out of the darkness of the drug abuse scene. I was taken to the crazy house after having a bad trip from PCP. Stayed in there for I know about two weeks or so, not knowing who I was, where I was, where my children were, or who had them. I was in a fog, as I stated, in a very dark, dark place and I couldn't get myself out. Just totally out of my mind at this point.

I felt I was losing my mind all over again with this happening to my babies. Only this time it was something that happened in the church. Please understand. I'm not putting the church down. The devil is a faithful member of everyone's churches, ministries, and families. Just like the Lord uses people, the devil uses people as well.

I had opened up myself again, trusting, trusting, trusting flesh! My flesh! His flesh! As a result, my babies were hurt...in the church.

Apostles, pastors, prophets, and leaders who operate in these gifts, sometimes the devil can use these very gifts himself. Remember, the Bible states gifts and callings of

God are without repentance. A lot of times the hit that's the most devastating hit in life is the one that you don't see coming, the sucker punch. The one you're not looking for. I was seeing the gifts more than I was seeing God. Lord, help me as I write.

Can anybody relate to my story? I feel like God is changing something for somebody in this season. As you continue on this journey with me, receive your breakthrough and healing. The spirit of the living God is here for you now! Miracles are happening now as you read. Let those tears flow! I am your voice! Release him and them out of your heart. Forgive and forget. Now take a praise break right here before you go any further! Lord, I thank You for my voice! Lord, I thank You that You're setting me free from this stronghold now! Thank You, Jesus, for my freedom!

Back to the first preacher, pastor, prophet I was referring to. We were only supposed to be in that ministry for a little while under watch care because we had no transportation to get from Los Angeles to Pasadena. Before we went, my sister and I asked permission from our pastor to attend the other ministry. It was never intended to be a long stay. Our overseer said, "Yes, you can go." The pastor told us, "I feel that I've taught you enough that if things are not right y'all will come up out of there." So, he said, "Yes, I release you to go."

Being under the leadership of a prophet, you would have thought that he could see all of this that was going to happen beforehand. But I also learned that the Lord doesn't always show us everything or tell us everything in advance. So being released, we went.

I wasn't the only victim there, I later heard. So many other women, daughters, and even sons, were affected by this lascivious spirit he would call "the spice of life." He preyed on the weak; and the fact that he was young and handsome didn't help. Every single, saved woman (Daddy's little girls) wanted a saved, anointed, powerful man of God. Some who were married also fell into that vortex web as well. I really didn't think I would make it out of that one. Some didn't. I actually prayed that the Lord would make sure I was saved and take me to heaven because I couldn't protect my girls from the wolf that was in sheep's clothing.

It was all my fault because I didn't take heed to the warning of the vision that was given to me while praying. I had awakened abruptly. I could feel my heart beating rapidly, but I couldn't move. All I could move was my head from side to side at the time. It was as if the rest of my body had absolutely no function at all. In the position that I was in, I could see my outer window. In the middle of the window were three figures. Their heads were attached together like that head of a hybrid. (The meaning of hybrid is the offspring of two plants or animals of different species or varieties, such as a mule, a hybrid of a donkey and a horse.) These three were the head of a child being goofy, the next was the head of a howling wolf, and the last one the head of a smiling cobra snake with a face. They were OUTSIDE of the window. None could harm me in any way.

After seeing these three images, I was allowed to go back to sleep. I couldn't wait to tell my sister, Alberta, who was staying with me at the time, what had happened and what I had seen. She was a notable example to me concerning holiness. Alberta listened and said, "The Lord is opening your eyes more in the realm of the spirit." When she told me this, I was like a little kid in a candy store. I had so much joy because the Lord was dealing with me like He did with others spiritually. I was overwhelmed with it all. Listen to me as you read, I never thought about it much after that until my girls and I went through that lust spirit experience that was in the preacher man.

He had told his testimony of how he had once had a pimping spirit and had gotten rid of it, supposedly, but ~ Not. I should have recognized it, being the praying woman that I was, but I guess it was hidden very well. You know the Word of God says to the pure all things are pure, and I really wasn't looking for it either. I felt that I was sent there to intercede for him and the church, which was filled with young adults who really didn't know God, nor did they have a real relationship with God, but I discerned enough to know that their relationship was with him. Even though lust and perversion were all around me growing up – they were on my family tree, in my DNA – still they were hidden, incognito at this time.

After this horrific episode with my daughters had taken place, it looked like that should've been the perfect reason to leave Christ and the church, but not even that was enough to make me deny my Lord. As I was riding the bus one day after everything, as my mother would say, had hit the fan, I began to ask God why? Why would He let something like that happen to me, His faithful servant? I'm saved, in the church, running after Jesus, living holy. Why? I wasn't even comparing mother's situation with mine. My focus was on me and my children.

I was broken, bruised, betrayed, and full of regret. I didn't know what to do because this situation was somehow different from any other test in my walk with God. In my mind I thought, he should die for the damage he had done just to me alone. Not even for all the rest of the women who fell into the trap of seduction and even some of the young men as well. Lust has no boundaries.

I found out later, after being in prayer, the Lord spoke to me and said, "Lorraine, if you had only sought me for the vision of the three spirits, you would have found out that these three spirits were that of one man ~ (Prophet _____). Names are not important – just the spirits. He had a spirit of a playful, retarded, goofy child; he had the spirit of a wolf in sheep's clothing, and last, the head of a cobra snake with a face belonging to him. The Holy Ghost was telling me that these three spirits wanted to get into the house, but because I didn't enquire of the Lord what the vision meant, I didn't seek God for the revelation, those spirits came into my family with a vengeance. Wow! What a hard lesson to learn, along with a hard way to learn it. God has His way in all things.

Finding how to turn my 'pain into passion' for others was not easy. I guess that's the reason we have the scripture, *"And we know that all things work together for good to them that love the Lord and are the called according to his purpose"* (Romans 8:28). One of the enemy's tricks was to get me to hating the preacher so much that it would bring me to a spirit of murder and to think the same thing about all men of the cloth. But the spirit of the Lord had given me another heart that I could pray honestly for him/them without any reservations. Thank God for prayer.

Reset

My former pastor had been in an afternoon service in Los Angeles, California, not too far from where I was staying. Not having a car, I walked to the church along with a friend of mine who was an evangelist. The service was high with that Pentecostal charismatic feel of the anointing. The man of God was on fire in the Spirit. Prophesy was going forth in the atmosphere. The Word of God was right on point as usual.

As I sat there waiting for him to call me out and tell me what I was expecting for him to know, he never did. People, what you need is not in a man or woman used by God but all you need is in God the Father who will never fail you.

Well, the prophetic Word of God didn't happen for me during the service. After the service was over my sister and I went up to the prophet like so many did. As soon as I walked up to him to shake his hand, he looked into my eyes and said, "Daughter, you have to come home now." I knew he meant back home to our church where he pastored in Pasadena. He said, "Sister So-and-So may stay a little while longer, but you have to come now." Now I had prayed the night before I went, and I had told the Lord if this is the way I have to live my life, then Lord, please make sure I'm saved and take me on home. That same sister was standing close by and heard what the prophet said to me. She then said, "Oh no, I can't stay there any longer either." Consequently, we packed our bags, so to speak, and went back to our former church in the beautiful city of Pasadena, CA, where my healing began to take place. But I didn't learn from that trial. I trusted again.

How Could This Happen in the Church?

Chapter 9

WHERE, OH WHERE IS MY DELIVERANCE?

Back to the church...Remember the man of God that I introduced you to in chapter 1? Now is the time for me to share the full story of that perverse illusion with you.

While I was patiently waiting for the man that I had fallen so deeply for, I found that this was not just a neutral contest, but it was an international contest that I was in, vying for his promise and commitment to marriage with me.

Because of his renowned gift, the Lord would send him all around the world. He was always on the go (revivals and such).

Most of you wouldn't think it strange that the other women in the church were at one point all friends, but now they can't seem to be able to stand one another's presence overnight. Can anybody see what the devil is doing up in here? Because now there's a new kid on the block, they're mad dogging each other.

One of my precious sisters actually found a pair of my eyeglasses in the room of my secret lover. She asked me if the glasses were mine. My answer was, "Yes ma'am, they are." Sister Jolly didn't care to take it any further, thank

God. Mind you, Sister Jolly, who was so interested, had her own husband and was considered trustworthy and saved.

He had this one sister in the mix who would cook for him. Don't get me wrong. Sister Jellybean cooked quite well. But so did some of the rest of the women. She wasn't his wife, but she just happened to be his favorite. Jellybean was so personal that he would stop at her house to watch the games and take along some of the brothers as well. Guess what? No one questioned anything.

Sister Jellybean didn't like me at all, and frankly I tried to care and get along. But Sister Jellybean was going to let everyone know that she was going to be the next. At all of our church meetings she would make sure that her seat was right by the preacher. She was appointed to cook on every fast, bringing him his special meal. She also held other important positions as well. Thus, you could see why she was so close, not being the wife, but personal enough for the closeness with him.

There were others who did special favors as well. I'm sure that most of them were innocent enough.

I was praying and fasting, trying to be healed, but it's different now over here in the holiness church. Right? What I used to do in the world was alcohol, drugs, and sex. Now, I feel every pain with no suppression. Oh Lord, how could I have fallen for that one kiss that always leads to hurt again and again? With that one kiss, there was a transference of spirits, disappointment, and more pain and heartache.

A few years went by as I continued to serve the people and the pastor. But when I got pregnant by the pastor, I felt like the bottom had fallen out of my world. No, not me, the praiser, warrior, intercessor, evangelist! No, not me, the one who's always at the church, singing, taking care of the mail, and running errands! Pregnant, with NO HUSBAND, AGAIN AT 40 YEARS OF AGE. Who me? Couldn't be...But because I loved God more than life, I kept it a secret as to who the father was, and I continued to believe the promises that he was going to marry me.

We would do ministry together as if there was no personal relationship going on. The one thing I didn't want was for the devil to use me to destroy the church. I didn't want the blood of the saints to be on my hands. Not only did I stay in the church, but I stayed quiet.

We continued the relationship for the next 18 years. I was stuck, fighting in the spirit with all the other wanna-be's waiting on the same man. Listen, the spirits of lust, pride, betrayal, fornication, adultery, seduction – you name it – they were prevalent, and they didn't care what my title was. My title didn't keep me from falling. All demons want is to please their master, Satan. In fact, they want us who are apostles, prophets, evangelists, pastors, and teachers more, because we are to edify the body of Christ, build the church up, and reconcile men, women, boys, and girls back to God. If the devil can make you fall, then those who are looking up to you most are likely to fall as well, especially if they don't have a personal relationship with God. Many look at their leaders as their gods.

So, I stayed there, silently waiting to do the right thing, sitting in the pews, watching, hurting, trusting. Now, to add salt to an open wound, ladies, here comes the baby, and the lies continue. No father in the open; just me. But in private, girls, he was there like no others had ever been. He was so different from any other man I had ever known in my life, so I thought. Sweeter than sweet. When I say one in a million, that was him. Sometimes even before I asked for it, anything the baby needed, anything I needed, anything my family needed, if it was in his power, it was there. But no ring and no commitment. Not even a promise ring. Really? The perfect man, father, and friend – who or what woman wouldn't want a man like that? Provider, warrior in prayer. The mouthpiece of God. COME ON!

Please don't get me wrong. I'm not playing the blame game. My mama always said, "It takes two to tango." What I'm saying is that a spirit of lust and perversion was already on my family tree. Little Milton wrote a song back in the day titled "Just One Kiss." That's what happened to me on that dark and lonely night, sitting there in his car with no one else around. What that one kiss did was unleashed a sleeping giant that was hard to put back to sleep – my flesh had been awakened. Seventeen years in what I called good standing with the Lord, and all of a sudden, as the Bible says, "you did run well, but who did hinder you?"

Why am I sharing in such great detail? Because all of these things were a direct attack against his character, leadership, and ministry; against my character, leadership, and ministry; and against the church itself. This was a master plan designed for the devil to use to destroy the church. But he forgot that the Word of God said that the gates of Hell shall not prevail against God's church. The devil tricked mother Eve in the garden, not Adam. The woman deceived the man. Trust.

Now, after the baby came, there was another test. Come on warriors, depending on your level of maturity, you will sometimes go through back-to-back trials. Remember, the Word says, *"Many are the afflictions of the righteous, but"* (thank God for the "but") *"the Lord will/shall deliver them out of them all"* (Psalm 34:19). It also says, *"A righteous man will fall seven times and rise up again"* (Proverbs 24:16). This is not written to be used to assassinate anyone's character, but to give many of you a voice. IT AIN'T OVER!

Even after the baby was born, he was afraid to come to the hospital for fear that he may have been recognized as her father. So, he called my sister and asked if the baby looked like him.

Gifts, Callings, and 'The Baby': 20 Years a Slave

I couldn't get rid of the baby because the Lord showed me in my eighth week her little heartbeat and He also told me on that table that the life was in the blood. Glory! My baby was blessed in it all, to grow up in the church, being a part of the youth department, praising and magnifying the Lord like nobody's business. I gave her my last name rather than the last name of her real father.... SECRETS!

When she was about maybe six or seven, she came to me and asked me, "Mama, who is my daddy?" because she was seeing her nieces and nephews all around her age had their fathers right there in the open for all to see. But hers was in the shadows. When I looked into those big brown eyes of hers, I knew I could not lie to her anymore. Maybe I should have, but I just couldn't. I told her that it was our little secret.

Now, having to grow up watching him recognize all his other children, but not her, was devastating. We sat in that church Sunday after Sunday and all through the week, and watched, like she and I weren't there. In private only was she his baby girl. The pain of being rejected was present and that spirit I knew right well. I would literally cringe for years as I too watched and listened at how proud he was of the children of his families from his different marriages. You say that would have been the part to make me go berserk. But sometimes you can't run. You have to go through it to get to it – the place in life the Lord has prepared for you. THE FIRE! THE PROCESS! I wondered if it would ever end.

Every time I wanted to leave the church, I heard the spirit of the Holy Ghost say to me, "Lorraine, if you want this anointing you have to pay for it. You can't run from this." He (the Lord) would not allow me to hide or to cover up my sin. The Bible says in Proverbs 28:12, 13, *"When the (uncompromisingly) righteous triumph, there is great glory and celebration; but when the wicked rise (to power), men hide themselves. He who covers his transgressions will not prosper, but whoever confesses and forsakes his sins will obtain mercy"* (see also Psalm 32:3, 5 and 1 John 1:8-10).

This price was being humiliated. Stop. What does it mean to be humiliated? The word, *humiliate,* means to make (someone) feel ashamed and foolish by injuring their dignity and self-respect, especially publicly. Yes, and if I hadn't had the prayer life I had when it happened ~ Jesus is the Lord.

I continued to fast; I continued to pray. I was even given a front row seat in the church for more than three years or so. I continued to go to the church. I continued to serve in whatever capacity I could. It sounds foolish but I am your voice. My older children would be wondering why Mama was always going to the altar. Man looks on the outward appearance, but God looks at the heart. My heart was crying out loudly, but yet there was no sound. No one could hear it but the Lord. My thoughts were always...I didn't come over here to go to hell from the church ~Help! I've fallen and I can't get up! I can't get up! I can't get free!

Did the Lord ever answer? Sure, He did, but in His own timing, after 20 years of bondage in the house of God. Twenty years? Yes, 20 years. You have to be careful about what you say that you would never do.

There was a time once in my life I couldn't understand why a young lady I knew was so in love and attached to a man she knew and loved since her childhood. He was a singer, a married man, also, and a friend of the family. She ended up having two children by him, and even though they were not together, she found herself stuck in an ungodly soul tie for 39 years to this church-going whoremonger. She would say, "Rain, I don't know why. I know he's no good, but I love him." Sound familiar? Thirty-nine years. I didn't get it. I said, "Girl that would NEVER be me." I was completely void of understanding the spirit world. No compassion or sympathy whatsoever. Years later when that situation knocked on my door... I let him in. It was hard to get him back out. You might say no not me, not this child. Well, keep on living.

When the Lord answered, did He answer the way that I had expected all those wonderful, horrible years? No. We had gone one night to the hospital to pray for one of my sisters who was gravely ill. I happened to suggest to him that we needed to get married, which I had mentioned countless times down through the years. The wife had died. Oh, did I mention that he had been married during that time? Just in case I didn't, he was. What's the excuse now? No offense. He answered me that night, "God is going to work it out." Yeah, but how much longer? I didn't want to go to hell from the church! So, I said, "Okay, we can go get married and still not tell anyone until you get ready. Then we will be blessed in our union." To cut to the chase, he agreed. "That's a very good idea."

Two years later I was tired! Finally. I was watching him being so up close and personal with his secretaries. I dropped him off at his hotel where he was staying at the time. Excuse my language; I was pissed off. I pulled off in the car and went home. I humbled myself and repented for my anger, as I had done so many times before. We continued as usual in silence, in secret. Finding myself still with no voice, trusting in flesh, watching, praying, trusting, waiting on him. Jesus.

Well, the next year, 2015, I didn't get a chance to go to the annual convention (because of money) like I had all of the other previous years. As all the people gathered from all over the country, the Lord did not allow me to go that particular year. He had made no provision for me as he had all the other years. He called saying, "I wish you could be here," really concerned. "I just don't have the money this year. My finances are crazy." Me... "Aww, it's alright sweetheart, I'm praying." While we were yet talking on the phone, he happened to say, "There she is." I said, "There who is?" He replied, "(his daughter's name); it's just Mother Grapetree." He repeated her name again. But I felt something in my stomach that wasn't right.

During this time, my baby sister was dying from lung cancer in hospice in my home. I continued praying, waiting on the Lord to work a miracle and raise my sister,

Angela, from her sick bed. However, my baby sister passed away.

I don't know how it leaked out, but someone said, "Reverend is married!" Then it got back to me. The man I'd been waiting for all these years is now married and had been married for two years already – While he was STILL WITH ME! Folks, when I say prayer makes the difference, please believe me. I found out it was the Lord who didn't let me attend the convention that year because He was about to expose and uncover the deception.

What is the point of all this? It is to remind you again – NO ONE is exempt from the attack of the devil. While the devil has many of you stuck on 'AIN'T NOBODY SAVED,' listen to how the Lord went on a mission, just to bring me out of this horrific cycle and into His divine purpose as His true intercessor.

What did the Lord do to bring me out of this devastating severe shock of distress and grief? He made me PRAY for THEM with all honesty and sincerity. (The word, *sincerity,* means the quality of being free from pretense, deceit, or hypocrisy). I cried my heart out, but I prayed and prayed and prayed. I said, like many of you, "Lord, why me?" I wouldn't wish this on my very worst enemy. I prayed some more.

Where, Oh Where Is My Deliverance?

I got to the point where I couldn't stand to hear his voice or his name, look at him on his television programs, look at any of his tapes, videos, or anything! I found myself sinking into deep depression. Life's mission seemed to be impossible for me to continue, but it wasn't impossible for God. I don't know exactly how long it was that I cried and prayed.

I thank God for my children and for my sister Precious (Brenda), who knew about the whole entire relationship with us. As far as I knew, she never put me (us) down. She never stopped looking at me as a woman of God or a sister, nor him as a man of God. She kept my secrets.

Well, the Lord kept me on the floor in my prayer closet. I cried from the depth of my soul. I didn't know if I was crying because of the loss of my baby sister or crying because of the loss of my secret lover. But all I know is that the pain was unbearable.

Chapter 10

MAKING PROGRESS

When I was a little girl my mother had given me a song to sing, written by the famous Staples Singers and titled "Pray on My Child." I wonder if my mom had an insight that one day I would be one of the Lord's chief intercessors and prayer warriors? Or would you even think that the Lord would call ME to such an office? In writing this book I am remembering the scripture that says all souls are God's.

The Effectual Fervent Prayer

There are so many people who don't pray effectively, just as I didn't. I really didn't know how to pray. Pastor Shirley Caesar once said in one of her songs that she wanted the Lord to teach her what to say. This is done by the Holy Spirit, according to Romans 8:26. I found out that prayer is not a hard thing to do; it's actually very simple. Prayer is simply talking to God. Jesus directed the disciples to pray, *"Our Father which art in heaven, hollowed be thy name. Thy kingdom come, thy will be done, on earth as it is in heaven. Give us this day our daily bread, and forgive us our debts as we forgive our debtors, and lead us not into temptation, but deliver us from evil: For thine is the kingdom, and the power, and the glory, forever. Amen"* (Matthew 6:9-13). Believe it or not there is so much power in that prayer alone. Simple but powerful. Start there if you don't know how to pray.

Now, I've always known that there was something special about prayer and the Word of God, even as a very young child. But I didn't know exactly what it was or what the Bible said concerning prayer. I learned quickly, though. I can recollect that as a child I was always seemingly getting into trouble like some little children do. Trouble should have been one of my legal names. There were times when I would get caught for being hard-headed. Man! I knew that when my mom got a hold on me... She would say, "Rain, give your heart to God, and your a#% to me."

I knew that there was something in that special book called the Bible that could save me. Believe it or not, when my mom would look over at me with that Bible in my hands as I would grab it, looking seriously into the Word of God, ACTING like I was reading it with such fascination, all of a sudden, Mom would have mercy on my little soul and let me go. She would just turn around as if the Lord Himself was talking to her, saying, "Leave her alone this time." I just knew every time that would be the one to get me out. I knew that I'd be on my way to meet my Maker due to my antics and behavior. I would go into the bathroom and pray a simple prayer: "Lord, please don't let Mama whoop me." Thank you, Lord; I got by again but not always away.

In my day, your parents could beat the spit out of you. They'd beat the skin off of your back because they knew you weren't going to die. There was no child abuse in many cases or police telling you that you couldn't whoop your children, for good reason, of course; or for the neighbors not to whoop your butt as well. They literally believed in the saying, "I brought you here and I'll take you away." It may have seemed harsh, but there was not a lot of us who were disrespectful to our elders anywhere, whether on the streets or in our neighborhoods.

So, I didn't get away with much, but there were times when something within me would prompt me to pray or to get around our small coffee table that was our altar. Mom would go into intercessory prayer right there. When she would start we just simply listened to her pray. As children, we didn't know the various levels that there are in prayer. Mom would call everyone's names out that she knew. I didn't know that was a part of intercession then, picking people up in the spirit. Of course, I would try to repeat everything she would say. She would look at me with understanding eyes and say to me, "No, Rain. Just be quiet and listen."

Training

Transformation. Perhaps you have heard that faith comes by hearing and hearing by the Word of God. I didn't know that there was an impartation going on in the realm of the spirit as I loved, not liked, but loved, to hear my mother pray. Most likely, your children will follow your example more than your advice.

Now one thing about prayer: It can bring the anointing of God upon you. Prayer brings joy into your soul; prayer also brings liberty. I kept noticing at that tender age that there was something about this prayer thing. There is so much power in prayer even when all you can do is moan.

Mom would gather her children together every Sunday morning around our little coffee table, which sat in the living room, in our small rear house. That was where the family altar was. The altar. Praying through the altar. Every home and every believer should have an altar for intercessory prayer. Remember, we ourselves didn't pray, but we learned to be in agreement while Mom would pray. It was just something about how Mom would talk to the Lord that was so amazing and fascinating to me. It would seem as though as I watched her weeping and wailing, it was like Jesus Himself was kneeling around that little coffee table with us. Even in this little humble place, when Mom would cry out to the Lord, or when she would sing, the very power of God would saturate that entire room. The Lord would always show up for those precious tears she shed.

The mantle of my mom fell to me. I'm writing this book because God's people all over the world need to know more about prayer and the deliverance, healing, and salvation that can come forth through the power of prayer. The more we know and learn, the more we need to know, because our adversary the devil is cunning and subtle. So many people want to know how to pray effectively, but don't know how. I've always known that there was something about praying and the Word of God but didn't know exactly what I was doing nor what was in the Holy Bible. And, I knew nothing about the Holy Ghost as our helper.

The Anointing

Back then, when the anointing would come upon people, church folk would say that the people were just getting happy. They would jump up and shout, swinging their arms and shaking profusely, shaking their heads, clapping their hands, and some would just rock back and forth and cry. It was really something to see. Most of the time in the Baptist church I grew up in, when the women would get too happy they would feel the cool air of a fan and that was enough to calm them down. If that didn't work, some of the deacons would literally pick them up and take them outside of the church until they regained their composure to come back in. This was done as a method to bring a sense of calmness back into the church. The Bible tells us not to quench the Spirit of God.

Now-a-days, we find that even in the Pentecostal sanctified churches, the devil wants it to seem sometimes like having the Holy Ghost is some mysterious talking to God. Many times, this can be because we don't know that the Lord wants to talk to us in prayer in secret. We sometimes don't know or understand that it can and will equip us for the different tests and situations that life will bring forth, or how it could empower us as believers, or that it takes work for it all to operate in sync.

We have to learn to pray the Word of God back to Him. The Bible says to put Him in remembrance of His word, of what He said. John 15:7 says, *"If my word abide (live) in you then you can ask the Father whatever you will, and it shall be done for you of my Father who is in heaven."* You have to work the Word and the Word will work for you. Jesus said in Luke 18:1 that men ought always to pray, and not to faint. Why would He say, "and not faint?" Well, in Strong's Concordance (G1573), the word, *faint,* means not to lose heart, or when tempted not to give up.

Growing up, we weren't taught a lot about the anointing. Some of the people would say things like, "Sister So and So sho' got happy today. Some of the sisters would cry out in a loud voice with a long, "YES SIRRRRRRR!" That was when the praise couldn't be controlled. Some would say, not knowing that the Lord was at work breaking down some strongholds, "Lord that's enough! You're messing up our program! Here you go, Sista," handing her a drink of water with a fan in the other hand. "We got you. You're doing a little too much. Please sit down suga and be quiet until we're ready for another praise break from you" (where we want it and not where the Spirit of the living God wants it). Thank you, Lord, for my Baptist heritage.

Now, in mostly all of our churches, the devil has stolen our cry and our ability to pray, as well as pray through. So, what is prayer? Prayer is an invocation or act that seeks to activate a rapport with an object of worship through deliberate communication. In the narrow sense, the term refers to an act of supplication or intercession directed towards a deity (a god), or a deified ancestor.

The Purpose of the Experience

I remember I asked the Lord one day why I had to go through all the hell I went through in the world (Egypt or Pharaoh's house, as I call it). Sound familiar? The Spirit of the Lord said to me that everything I went through there, was for someone else in here (meaning in God's house) as well as someone out there (still in the world). You might be reading this book right now and wondering how, when, and what happened that landed you in captivity, and caught up by the game? It was all for you. I had to feel, learn, and have compassion on the souls that God has destined for me to reach. I had to let you and everyone else know that they weren't the only ones who had made a wrong decision or a wrong turn in life. God knows your struggles and your pain, and my experiences allow me the opportunity to identify with your issues and to let you know there is a way out through Christ! He delivered me and He can do the same for you!

I see so many now in the body of Christ who feel like they have arrived and are ready for heaven ~ Not. They've forgotten that it took the blood of Jesus when they were in their horrible pits to wash away their sins. Many have forgotten what it was like being young trying to find your identity and looking for love in really all the wrong places. Now they think they're here to look down on others ~ Not.

Lord, help me today (SMH). Therefore, embrace the hardships, troubles, heartaches, etc. God has a plan, and all things are working together for your good.

Even when you don't understand the WHY'S, the Word of the Lord tells us, *"Trust in the Lord with all your heart and lean not to your own understanding. In all your ways acknowledge Him and He will direct your path"* (Proverbs 3:4, 5). Romans 8:28 tells us, *"And we know that all things work together for the good of them that love the Lord and are the called according to his purpose."*

Have you ever asked yourself that question – "Who am I?" Or, "Why am I here in the earth realm? My life is a mess. I've got so many secrets...even some beyond the pews! God couldn't love me or need me for His plan and purpose...I'm just not good enough."

So, the battle is within. You feel that you're not up for the task, but you tolerate the lies and pursue the passionate amounts of sexual gratification, holding nothing back, wrapped up, tied up, tangled up in this web of destruction. Author Sonya Parker summed it up this way: "Bad relationships are like a bad investment – no matter how much you put into it you'll never get anything out of it. We need to find someone that's worth investing in!"

Making Progress

Chapter 11

SEXUAL ETHICS ISSUES

Pastors may not be more vulnerable to sexual sin than anyone else, but they are probably not less vulnerable either, in my honest opinion. Certainly, their unique calling puts them "in harm's way" more than others. Why? Consider three factors, two of which are uniquely attached to the work of ministry.

1) Not too many people can pass by a billboard or turn on the television without encountering strong sexual signals nowadays.

2) Pastors and leaders are not immune to their influences.

3) The typical church ministry can often strain a marriage through long, erratic hours; emotionally charged situations; a sense of isolation; and close encounters with people who are searching for companionship, strength, and tenderness, some of whom may make themselves too available for a sexual relationship.

I did not know all the tricks of Satan with leaders. One of the facts about spiritual battles is, *"Strike the shepherd and the sheep will be scattered"* (Zechariah 13:7).

Only God Himself knows how many ministries are crippled, how many congregations are split, how many non-believers are hardened against the gospel, how many Christians grow disillusioned, and how much work in God's kingdom is thwarted, all because ministers fall into sexual sin. Few weapons in Satan's arsenal are more effective in attacking the work of God than bringing down a church leader. You must guard vigilantly against sexual temptation. If you think you're immune to temptation in this area, you must particularly guard against it!

Pain Is Necessary

If you've ever endured sleepless nights and agonizing days because of unending pain, you're acutely aware of the following reality: we weren't designed for this! While in Eden, our ancestors experienced a life free of pain, insecurity, and anxiety. Life wasn't meant to be this way! However, pain and negative emotions are essential to draw our attention to God and things eternal. At the close of his dialogue with God about suffering, Job stated, *"My ears had heard of you but now my eyes have seen you"* (Job 42:5).

Even death is necessary outside of Eden. Without it, we would be doomed. We have to learn to turn our pain into passion. We need to use our painful situations to impact others. I'm learning to use the leftovers, as Jesus salvaged the leftovers, and there was even more to spread around. Our strength is in our ruins.

Where do our negative thoughts come from? We have to find the root or the entry point of the thing. Who did the devil use to speak or loose the spirit of negativity over you, that you begin to live that thing? The devil works in that mindset.

Take your pain and from there, get your truth out of it. Sometimes you have to talk to yourself and speak over yourself in the Lord. Renew your mind. Feed your hope and starve your fears. We act, talk, and speak according to wholeness or to brokenness. Don't hide; continue to show up with your broken pieces that God can make whole. Tell the devil you are not his playground.

Prayer changes not only things, but prayer will also change your location. It takes you from the natural world to the spirit world. This world is full of broken people and the Lord needs you and me to help put these broken people back together again with His Word.

Our focus should always be on the Lord. Philippians 4:6 says, *"Do not be anxious about anything, but in every situation by prayer and petitions with thanksgiving, present your requests to God. And the peace of God, which transcends all understanding, will guard your hearts and your minds in Christ Jesus."*

"Why Buy the Cow?"

Mama used to say, "Why buy the cow when you can get the milk for free?" As Daddy's little girls, we need to remember all those old sayings that many of us have forgotten about in the church and out. They didn't make a lot of sense then, but...

Why get married when you can have marriage privileges, yet with NO COMMITTEMENT, NO DEMANDS, or NO STRINGS ATTACHED? Here's what both parties are saying. "I can stay as long as I want to stay and also leave whenever I please." They're not thinking that there are these soul ties being created, one after another.

Let me reiterate a few verses in 1 Corinthians 6. Verse 12: *"Everything is permissible for me, but not all things are beneficial. Everything is permissible for me, but I will not be ENSLAVED by anything (and brought under its power, allowing it to CONTROL ME)."*

Pause; I didn't write this book just to tickle your fancy, to make you say, "Oooooh I knew it, I knew it. I told you ain't nobody saved." Well, when you read the Bible, you will find out that ALL HAVE SINNED AND COME SHORT OF THE GLORY OF GOD. So, you who are without sin,

CAST THE FIRST STONE. Verses 13-15: *"Food is for the stomach and the stomach for food, but God will do away with both of them. The BODY is not intended for sexual immorality, but for the Lord, and the Lord is for the body (to save, sanctify, and raise it again because of the sacrifice of the cross). And God has not only raised the Lord (to life) but will also raise us up by his power. Do you not know that your bodies are members of Christ?"*

Come on, Daddy's little girls. Let's take a stand. NO MORE FREE MILK! LET HIM BUY THE COW! Your pain is no longer your own. You can release, repent, and renew your strength. No matter what has happened, the enemy has no more control over you...

Be healed, be delivered, be whole!

NO MORE SECRETS...

Sexual Ethics Issues

AUTHOR'S BIOGRAPHICAL SKETCH

Apostle Lorraine Anderson was born in Southern California. She is an ordained minister of the gospel of Jesus Christ, according to St. Luke 4:18. Even at the tender age of 9 years old in the Baptist church, the Spirit of the Lord would come upon her mightily when she would sing. All the elders of the church knew that the hand of the Lord was upon her life. They perceived the Lord would use her one day. As a young girl, Apostle Lorraine would always play church with her sisters. Of course, she would always end up mocking and being the preacher, always trying to get a laugh out of someone, but never guessing the Lord had said from her mother's womb that the last laugh would be on her. For truly it was the Lord who called her into the ministry, something that she really didn't want.

But for the past thirty years she has served under Prophet/Pastor Rogers G. DeCuir of the Holy Deliverance Pentecostal Church located in the beautiful city of Pasadena, California. Prophet DeCuir mentored her in the flow of the anointing of Esther, Deborah, Hanna, and Anna, who were biblical intercessors, and powerful women of God. She also operates in the anointing of Joseph, for she has been given a mandate to pray passionately and intensely for her family. Apostle Anderson has been trained and anointed to go forth in intense prayer, fasting, and deliverance.

She was also trained in various parts of the ministry such as the nurse's board, choir, administrative department for the ministry, praise and worship, usher's board, and the women's department, so she would know what it means to be a servant of God to His people. Apostle Lorraine has humbly and unpretentiously served and supported many other ministries down through the years.

The Lord has also given Apostle a tremendous burden for impacting women of all races and denominations, and to help heal their brokenness. The Lord also designed Apostle Anderson's ministry to empower, encourage, enrich, and birth out intercessors. She has learned the task of Godly counseling with a listening ear. Apostle Lorraine is also known to many as Mother Anderson, which is an honor to be trusted as a mother in Zion. Being made a spiritual mid-wife in the kingdom of God, Apostle Lorraine's desire is to reach the unreachable, untouchable, unsaved, unloved, and the ones who are the closest to hell's fire for all eternity. Her assignment is also to assist in the building of God's kingdom by winning souls for Christ by the spoken word of God by any means necessary. She demonstrates the power of God. One of her visions is to know that people's lives have been changed for the greater good. Apostle Lorraine has also ministered on several broadcast stations throughout the United States.

In 1999, Apostle Lorraine was given a certification of ordination by the Prayer and Share Ministries in the Worldwide Pentecostal Fellowship to preach the gospel by evangelizing and teaching, as well as to pastor. On November 22, 2003, she received an honorary Doctor of Divinity Degree given to her by the Mount Carmel Theological Seminary by Bishop John Sims, president.

In 2005, Apostle Lorraine founded the Beyond the Veil Church of Deliverance out of her home in Rialto, CA. There she pastored for about 3½ years until the Lord spoke to her to return home to her mother church in Pasadena under the leadership of her pastor, Bishop-Prophet DeCuir for another season of waiting for direction. Also, during that time, in 2005, the Spirit of the Lord gave her the assignment to bring His people back to their knees by taking prayer from city to city and state to state by starting the Wailing Wall International Prayer Ministry, the church with no walls, reaching those who were not getting a visit from the church as often as they could have. Therefore, the lifeline was formed.

On September 15, 2021, she was installed into the office of Apostleship by Chief Apostle Michael Hodges at the Holy Convocation, Triumphant Ministries International, Inc. But throughout this journey, if she's learned anything, she's learned most to DEPEND ON JESUS!

You can reach out to Apostle Lorraine Anderson at:

secretsbeyondthepews@gmail.com
wailingwallprayerministries@gmail.com,
or via office phone number: (682)422-9056

Or on Facebook:
https.www.facebook.com/lorraineanderson.92798